ROBO-RUNNERS
Tunnel Racers

www.damianharvey.co.uk

Books in the **Robo-Runners** series:

The Tin Man

Tunnel Racers

Razorbites

Powerball

The Ghost Sea

Aquanauts

ROBO-RUNNERS

Tunnel Racers

by **DAMIAN HARVEY**

Illustrated by **Mark Oliver**

h
Hodder
Children's
Books

A division of Hachette Children's Books

For my dad, Norman Harvey,

who shared a love of reading

Class No. _J._   Acc No. _C12227057._

Author: _Harvey D._   Loc: _13._

LEABHARLANN
CHONDAE AN CHABHAIN

Harvey D.

1. **This book may** returned on / be ow.
2. **A fine of 50c wil** part of week a book de 23)

At the edge of Metrocity lies an old junk yard where huge piles of scrap metal stretch as far as the eye can see. Pathways twist and turn their way between old spacecraft, wrecked land cruisers and machinery of all shapes and sizes.

The pathways are littered with rusting parts and small pools of oil and rocket fuel that's leaked from twisted pipes and damaged engine pods.

Into this maze of towering wrecks and torn metal came four robot friends, Crank, Al, Torch and Sparks, travelling in search of a safe place for old robots.

A place where robots are free to live their lives in peace.

A place called Robotika.

Leaving the recycling plant behind them, the four robots headed deeper into the junk yard. Some of the pathways were wide, but others were narrow, and the friends found themselves having to clamber over things or crawl through narrow gaps to get past.

Al was a young robot and should never have been taken to the recycling plant at all, but now he was finding it difficult to keep up with the others. Ever since the Tin Man had stolen his legs, Al had been forced to walk on his hands. He'd hoped to find some new legs in the junk yard, but so far they'd only come across one pair and they'd been too badly damaged. It looked as though *something* had been trying to eat them.

As the sun started to set, long, dark shadows crept across their path and Al kept looking round, peering nervously over his shoulder.

"Are you sure this is the right way?" he said.

"Of course I am," said Crank. "*Any* way that leads us away from the recycling plant must be the right way. Right?"

Al wasn't sure, but Crank *was* much older than him so perhaps he knew best.

"I suppose so," said Al. "But I do keep thinking we are going round in circles."

"Going round in circles!" laughed Crank. "How can we be going round in circles?"

"He's right," said Torch, the old Fire and Rescue robot, "we've gone past this engine pod five times already."

"Are you sure?" said Crank.

"Positive," said Torch. "I make a little mark on it each time we go past."

Crank looked closely at the

engine pod, and sure enough there were five little marks scratched on the side.

"Oh great," said Crank. "Why didn't you tell me?"

"I didn't like to mention it," said Torch. "Anyway, I thought we were looking for something."

"We *are* looking for something," said Crank. "We're looking for Robotika. A place where we can be free to live our lives in peace. But we'll never find anything unless we get out of this junk yard."

Crank sat down next to the engine pod and shook his head sadly. "We're *supposed* to be a team," he said. "If we're *ever* going to find Robotika we've got to work together. We've got to tell each other things. All right?"

Al and Torch nodded their heads, and Sparks, a spider-like engineering robot, beeped and whistled in agreement.

"Good," said Crank. "Well, let's get going."

"There's just one thing," said Torch.

"Now what?" cried Crank.

"Well," said Torch, "if we're telling each other things then I *should* tell you we're being followed."

"I knew it," said Al, hopping from hand to hand excitedly. "I *knew* there was something following us."

"Something following us?" said Crank. "Are you sure?"

"Oh yes," said Torch, "it's been following us since we came into the junk yard."

Crank looked around nervously. "Well!" he said. "What is it?"

"You don't want to know," said Torch. "Let's just keep walking."

"Of course I want know," said Crank. "I wouldn't have asked if I didn't want to know."

"Believe me," said Torch. "You *really* don't want to know."

"That's it," said Crank. "I've had enough of this. If you won't tell me what it is then I'll just have to find out for myself."

Crank turned round and started heading back in the other direction. "Come on," he shouted. "I know you're there … It's no good trying to hide. Come out and show yourself … We're not frightened of you."

"Oh yes we are," said Torch, backing away. "We're *very* frightened."

Crank stopped walking and froze to the spot with one foot in the air. He turned his head slowly and looked at Torch.

"What do you mean, we're *very* frightened?" he said. "Just what is it that's following us?"

"It's a dog," said Torch. "A guard dog."

"Oh, is that all?" said Crank. "I like dogs."

"Not this one you won't," said Torch. "It's a botweiler. One of the nastiest, most vicious robo-dogs ever made."

"Don't worry," said Crank. "I'm a robo-dog expert. You just need to know how to handle them. Watch and learn, my friend, watch and learn."

Crank picked up a metal bar from the floor and started walking back along the path. He hadn't gone far when something made him stop.

Standing in the middle of the path was a botweiler. It was the biggest robo-dog Crank had ever seen.

The botweiler was as tall as Crank. Its head, which seemed to be made entirely of teeth and eyes, was level with his face. The eyes were like silver ball bearings, cold and hard. They stared straight at Crank without blinking ... even the eye hanging from its socket on a piece of wire.

Crank stared back at the botweiler, hardly daring to move. He opened his mouth to speak but seemed to have forgotten how to. His mouth moved but no words came out.

"Good dog!" he finally managed.

In reply, the botweiler let out a metallic growl that sounded like a bucket of rusty nails being slowly crushed.

The robo-dog took a step forward and opened
its huge mouth, revealing rows of rusty, jagged
teeth.

Crank slowly took a step backwards.

"Use the metal bar," whispered Torch, from behind him.

Of course, thought Crank, *the metal bar*. He'd forgotten all about that.

The metal bar Crank had picked up was good and solid. It was thicker than his arm and as heavy as a sledgehammer. He could feel its weight in his hand.

As the botweiler came towards him, Crank slowly lifted the metal bar above his head.

"Go on," said Torch, "now!"

The botweiler growled once more and Crank swung the metal bar as hard as he could.

"Fetch!" shouted Crank, and let go of the bar, sending it spinning through the air high over the junk yard.

The botweiler didn't even blink. It opened its mouth wider and let out another growl.

"Right," said Crank. "I think we'd better ...

RUN!"
he shouted.
The others
didn't need telling
twice. Sparks and
Al were already racing
off between piles of
junk, and Torch wasn't far
behind them.

"Botweilers do *not* play fetch,"
cried Torch as they leaped over an
oil puddle.

"Well it works with other robo-dogs,"
shouted Crank, ducking beneath a row of
metal pipes.

"Botweilers are *not* normal robo-dogs," yelled
Torch, clambering up the side of an old spacecraft.
"You were supposed to knock its head off."

"I'll remember that next time," shouted Crank, overtaking Al and Sparks.

"With botweilers there is no next time," yelled Torch.

The four friends ran as fast as they could across the junk yard, twisting and turning, dodging and weaving, desperately trying to get away from the botweiler. Ducking beneath the wing of an old starglider, Crank was sure they had shaken it off. Then he came to a skidding halt – stopping so quickly that Torch ran straight into him.

Standing in front of them, in the middle of the path, was another botweiler.

The second botweiler was even bigger than the first, but this one shone like polished silver and its teeth were as long and sharp as knives. When it growled, the sound was deep and rumbling, echoing off the walls of scrap metal around them.

Crank turned and looked back the way they had come, but there was no escape there. The first botweiler had caught up and was walking slowly towards them with bared teeth and a rusty growl.

"Do something," hissed Crank.

"What can *I* do?" said Torch.

"Use your torch or something," said Crank, pointing at the dials on Torch's arm.

Torch pointed at the first botweiler and twiddled with the dials on his arm. There was a loud roar and a huge jet of flame shot out of the nozzle on the back of his wrist and engulfed the botweiler.

After a few seconds Torch turned the dial again and the jet of flame disappeared.

The botweiler growled and bared its teeth.

"Oh well done," said Crank. "Now you've *really* made it angry."

"I didn't think it would work," said Torch. "Botweilers are perfect guard dogs and they are almost indestructible. They've probably been here for years, guarding the junk yard against thieves."

"Thieves!" cried Crank. "But we're not thieves."

"I know that," said Torch, "... but they don't. Perhaps you could try telling them as they tear us apart."

Crank looked around desperately, hoping there might be a place to hide or even a weapon to use against the botweilers. But there was nothing.

Then a movement caught his eye.

In amongst the wall of junk that lined the pathway, a door had swung open and a huge, square-jawed robot with hands like shovels glared out at them.

"I fink you'd better duck," growled the huge robot.

Crank looked round in time to see the silver botweiler charging towards them. "Duck!" he yelled, and dropped to the floor, pulling Torch with him.

"Arghh!" screamed Al, falling flat on his back as the botweiler leaped into the air.

Crank saw a silver blur of teeth and claws, and heard the dog's terrible growl as it flew straight over them.

There was a startled snarl from the first botweiler as it tried to get out of the way, then an ear-splitting crunch as the second dog landed on it. For a moment the air was filled with snarling and the snapping of jaws as the two robo-dogs fought. Then with a final crunch and squeak of tearing metal, it was all over.

"Good boy, Scamp," growled the huge robot as it squeezed through the door in the wall of junk.

"Scamp!" laughed Crank. "Why do you call it Scamp?"

"Coz dat's his name," growled the huge robot as it lumbered towards them.

"Well my name's Crank," said Crank, getting to his feet. "And these are my friends, Torch, Al and Sparks."

The botweiler let out a deep growl and bared its teeth in warning as Crank and the others stood up.

"SIT!" roared the huge robot.

The four robots sat down again quickly.

"I woz talkin' to da dog," said the huge robot.

"Yes, we knew that," laughed Crank. "We were just having a rest."

"No time to rest," growled the huge robot. "It gettin' dark. Da rats will be comin'."

"Rats?" said Al, looking around nervously.

"Yeah!" growled the huge robot. "Stainless steel rats."

"They have teeth like bolt cutters," said Torch.

"Yeah!" growled the huge robot. "An' claws like razor blades."

"I've heard they could eat through your leg in the blink of an eye," said Crank.

"Dat's right," said the huge robot. "So you 'ad better come wiv me."

"Where are we going?" asked Al.

"We is going to da Workshop," said the huge robot.

"What workshop?" asked Crank.

The huge robot stopped for a moment and seemed to think hard about something before finally making up its mind.

For such a large robot it moved surprisingly quickly. Its hands were a blur as they reached out and grabbed Crank and Torch by the tops of their heads.

Before they knew what was happening the two robots were dangling in the air in front of the huge robot's face.

"You is not Engineerz, is you?" roared the huge robot suspiciously.

"No! No!" squealed Crank and Torch together. "Definitely not Engineerz!"

"Dat is all right den," growled the huge robot. "If you is not Engineerz, den you *must* be Mekanix."

Crank was about to say he'd never heard of the Engineerz or the Mekanix, but something told him this might be a bad idea.

"You is going to da Mekanix Workshop," growled the huge robot, putting Crank and Torch down again.

The huge robot picked up the broken botweiler, threw it on to one of the scrap piles and headed back towards the doorway. "Come on, Scamp," he growled. The silver botweiler ran past the four robot friends and disappeared through the doorway.

"Is you comin'?" growled the huge robot, getting ready to close the door. "Or is you stoppin' to play wiv da rats."

Crank didn't know who this huge robot was or what would happen when they reached the workshop ... but he did know it was getting dark. He could see tiny red eyes glowing in the shadows. The rats were coming out for the night and Crank definitely didn't want to be around when they started getting hungry.

"We're coming," said Crank, dashing towards the door. "Wait for us."

The four robots stepped through the doorway and into a narrow passage that went straight into one of the junk piles. The walls and ceiling were junk and the floor was littered with bits and pieces, making it hard to walk without tripping over.

Crank managed to make his way along the passage but found it was a dead end just as he heard the sound of the huge robot closing the door. It looked as though they were trapped in this tiny passageway.

"I'm starting to get a bad feeling about this," said Crank.

"Just where *is* this workshop?" said Al, backing along the passage.

"Grunt take you," said the huge robot.

"Grunt?" said Al. "What is Grunt?"

"I is Grunt," said the huge robot, rooting around on the floor.

"Grunt!" said Crank. "Why are you called Grunt?"

The huge robot stood still and thought for a moment.

"Coz dat is my name," he said, pulling open a large metal hatch in the floor. "We go dis way."

"Ah! A hidden doorway," said Crank. "I didn't see that."

"Dat is coz it woz hidden," said Grunt proudly. "And I is da one wot hid it."

As soon as the hatch was fully open, Scamp, the botweiler, leaped into the hole and disappeared.

"You is next," said Grunt, "but don't make a noise. If da Engineerz hear us dey will tear us apart."

"Tear us apart!" said Al. "Why would they do that?"

"Da Boss says dey is only caring about one fing," said Grunt. "Building da fastest tunnel racer. And dey would pull us apart just to get da bits dey need."

So as quietly as they could, the four robots lowered themselves down through the hatch and into the darkness below. The only light was coming from the open hatch and that disappeared as Grunt closed it with a deafening clang.

"Oops!" said Grunt as the noise echoed around in the darkness. "Sorry about dat."

As the echoes faded away another sound took its place.

Sparks whistled and beeped urgently.

"You are right," said Al. "It does sound like a lot of engines."

"It is da Engineerz," growled Grunt. "Dey is coming."

"Dis way," said Grunt, and headed off into the darkness with the four robot friends following close behind.

"Shouldn't we be going a bit faster?" asked Al. "The Engineerz might catch us."

"Nah," said Grunt. "I never seen da Engineerz round here for a long time. I only hears dem."

As they walked along, the sound of the Engineerz faded into the distance, and Crank realised that the tunnel wasn't as dark as he'd first thought. A long line of lights ran along the ceiling, giving off a faint glow. It wasn't bright enough to see anything properly, but Crank could just make out the shape of the walls and ceiling around them.

"Where are we?" he asked. "It looks like we're in a big tube."

"We is in da drains," said Grunt.

"Erghh!" cried Al. "Why are we in the drains?"

"Dat is where we live," said Grunt. "No one *ever* comes down here."

"I am not surprised," said Al. "I would not have come here if I had known."

"It is safe in da drains," said Grunt.

"But what about the rats?" said Torch.

"And the Engineerz?" said Crank.

"Well," said Grunt, thinking carefully, "apart from da rats and da Engineerz of course. But no one tries to crush you when you live in da drains. Robots is free down here."

"*What was that?*" said Crank excitedly. "Did you say robots are free down here ... free to do what they want?"

"Dat is right," said Grunt. "We is free to do anyfink we want."

"That's fantastic," said Crank. "Perhaps we've found Robotika already."

"No," said Grunt. "You av found da Workshop."

He stopped walking and turned round. "Ta-da!" he said. "What do you fink?"

The four robots looked around and then looked at each other.

"What do we think about what?" said Crank, scratching his head.

"Da Workshop of course," said Grunt.

Crank looked around again but all he could see was the tunnel disappearing into darkness. "What workshop?"

"Oh yeah!" said Grunt. "It's behind dis door."

Grunt rapped his giant knuckles against the side of the tunnel, making a deep booming sound that sent echoes chasing each other into the darkness.

Before the last of the echoes had faded away, a tiny door opened in the middle of the wall and the smallest, ugliest robot Crank had ever seen popped its head out.

"What do *you* want?" it squawked.

"Open da door," said Grunt.

"Says who?" squawked the little robot.

"Open sez me," growled Grunt, bending down to look at it. "Unless you wants me to pull your ugly little head off and use it as a—"

The little robot disappeared and the door snapped shut before Grunt had time to finish. Then, with a loud rumbling, a huge piece of the tunnel wall slid away to reveal a large doorway.

As soon as the door had opened there was a blur of movement from inside and something big and silver charged out and crashed straight into

Grunt. Crank turned and was about to start running back along the tunnel when a loud noise stopped him.

It was Grunt laughing.

"Hur, hur, hur … good boy," laughed Grunt, pushing the huge botweiler away with a playful shove that would have knocked a tree over. "He always gets home before me."

As Grunt walked through the doorway another robot jumped down in front of him and waved a spanner in his face.

"What are you doing here?" snarled the robot. "You're not supposed to come back until you've found a driver. Wait until the Boss finds out. He'll have your nuts and bolts for his supper."

Grunt grabbed the spanner out of the robot's hand and crushed it between two giant fingers. "I is back, coz I 'as found one," growled Grunt. "So you 'ad better get back to work and fix da racer."

Grunt stepped to one side and Crank, Al,

Sparks and Torch got their first view of the Mekanix Workshop.

"Dis is da garage," said Grunt.

Sparks let out a long whistle and stepped forward, eager to get a closer look at everything.

The garage was a big room but there was so much stuff packed inside that it appeared small and cramped. Round the outside of the room there

were workbenches, drills, cutting tools and piles of spare parts. There were even more tools hanging on the walls, and robots of all shapes and sizes were hammering, welding, cutting and generally busying themselves around the thing in the middle of the room.

When Crank saw what they were working on, he couldn't take his eyes off it.

"Wow!" he cried, stepping forward to get a closer look. "Just look at the wheels. Look at the engine. Look at the … er … other bits. It's amazing."

"Yes," agreed Al. "But what is it?"

"Dis is Da Beast," said Grunt. "It is da Mekanix tunnel racer."

Everything in the room suddenly went quiet and the Mekanix stopped working and stared at Crank.

Crank looked back at them and tried his best to smile, but there was something about the way they stared that made him nervous. The Mekanix had a strange, hungry sort of look on their faces and they were looking at Crank as though he were a big juicy steak.

"Er … hello," said Torch, trying his best to break the silence. "It looks like you're doing a really good job here."

None of the robots said anything.

"Why are they all staring at me?" whispered Crank.

"Coz dey knows you," said Grunt. "You is da driver, an' dey are da Mekanix. Dey av bin waiting for you."

"I'm the what?" said Crank.

Grunt didn't reply, but the Mekanix had started whispering to each other. Crank couldn't tell what they were saying at first but the whispering gradually got louder until it became a deafening shout. "DRIVER, DRIVER, DRIVER, DRIVER," they yelled.

Then, like a big metal wave, the robots ran straight at Crank.

"Aarghhh!" he squealed as the Mekanix washed over him and lifted him into the air.

Crank cried for help again but there was nothing the others could do against so many other robots.

All they could do was watch helplessly as the Mekanix carried Crank across the garage and out through the big doors at the far end.

"Stop them!" yelled Torch.

"You can't stop dem," said Grunt. "Dey is too excited. Nothin' can stop da Mekanix when dey gets excited."

"But what are they going to do with Crank?" asked Al.

"Dey is taking him to da Boss," said Grunt. "Da Boss will tell dem what to do."

"What about us?" said Al. "Why didn't they take us to see the Boss?"

"Dey is not excited about you," said Grunt. "You is not da driver."

"I could be a great driver," said Al.

"You do not understand," said Grunt, shaking his head. "Come on … Grunt will show you."

Sparks stayed where he was, busy peering into the Beast's engine, while Grunt led Al and Torch out through the big doors at the far end of the garage and into a wide tunnel. The tunnel curved away in both directions and there was no sign of the Mekanix, or Crank, but their shouts and yells could be heard echoing from round the corner.

"*We* is going in here," said Grunt, leading the two robots into another room.

The room was about the same size as the garage but it looked much bigger. Where every bit of space in the garage had been taken up with tools and spare parts, this room seemed almost empty. There was lots of space to walk round and look at things … though it was hard to tell what all the things were.

Along each wall there were moving video-pics of robots. Some of them showed robots waving at the camera, while others were sitting in race cars giving a thumbs-up or an OK sign.

One of the video-pics showed a robot waving his arms around madly. It seemed to be shouting at the camera, but as there was no sound Al couldn't tell what it was saying.

The very last one must have been faulty as the video-pic showed a worried-looking robot face for a few seconds but was then replaced by a fuzzy screen. Al

watched the image repeat itself a few times before going to join Torch, who was looking at a display table in the middle of the room.

"What do you fink?" asked Grunt.

"I think it looks marvellous," said Al.

"Yes," agreed Torch. "It looks fantastic."

The two robots stood for a few minutes looking at the display table before Al spoke again.

"It does look good," said Al.

"And so nicely set out," added Torch.

"But what is it?" asked Al.

"Dis is da Mekanix racing museum," said Grunt.

"Oh, I see," said Torch. "So all of these pictures are of racing drivers."

"Dat is right," said Grunt. "But dey is not just any old drivers. Dey is Mekanix drivers."

"And what are all these things on the table?" asked Al.

"Dey are some of da drivers as well," said Grunt.

"Drivers?" said Al, examining something that looked worryingly like a hand.

"Yeah," said Grunt sadly. "And dat piece is

extra-special. Dat is Pylon's left hand. He was our first champion."

Torch looked at the piece of robot hand that he'd been examining and carefully put it back on the display table. "So what happened to the rest of Pylon?" he asked.

"Pylon won da race," said Grunt. "So now he is da Boss."

"I see," said Torch. "But what is his hand doing here?"

"He had a little accident and we couldn't find da rest of his arms," said Grunt. "Or his legs."

"What about all these other bits and pieces?" said Al. "Are they all winners that have had little accidents too?"

"Oh no," said Grunt. "Most of dem woz losers. Da Mekanix get very upset with da drivers if dey lose."

"But what about Crank?" cried Al. "What are the Mekanix going to do to Crank?"

"Dey is going to look after him," said Grunt. "Coz Crank is da new driver."

"You mean *Crank* is going to be in a race?" said Al.

"Dat is right," said Grunt. "An' he will be da winner, and have his picture up on da wall. Coz he is just like da other winners."

"How do you know he will be the winner?" cried Al. "He could have an accident and—"

But Torch stopped him saying anything else and pointed up at the wall.

"Look at them," he said.

"This is no time to be looking at pictures!" cried Al. "We have to help Crank."

"But they are all ZX TK 60s," said Torch. "Just like Crank."

"Dat is wot I said," said Grunt. "Your friend is a winner. Dat is why da Mekanix is so excited. We av not had a winner for a long time."

"But what if he loses?" asked Torch.

"If he loses," growled Grunt, "dey will put his bits on a display to remind everyone."

"To remind everyone of what?" said Al.

"To remind everyone dat he lost," said Grunt.

"This is crazy," said Al. "Crank cannot go in the race. He has never even driven a race car."

"I think we'd better tell Crank what's happening," said Torch.

"Oh no," said Grunt. "You can't tell him anyfink. It will get him worried and you shouldn't worry da driver before da race."

"Why not?" asked Torch.

"Well," said Grunt, pointing at the faulty video-pic on the wall. "Flywheel got worried before his race, and ka-boom."

"Ka-boom?" said Al, looking puzzled. "What is ka-boom?"

"One minute he was there," said Grunt, "and da next minute ... KA-BOOM ...!"

"You mean he blew up?" cried Torch.

"Dat is right," said Grunt. "Now I fink it's time you met da Boss."

Grunt took Al and Torch in the same direction
that the Mekanix had taken Crank earlier, but
there was no sign of their friend or of the
Mekanix.

"Where did they go?" asked Al.

"Don't you worry," said Grunt. "You will see
dem soon enough."

"Wait a minute," said Torch. "Where's Sparks?"

"He was busy lookin' at Da Beast," said Grunt.
"He will be all right."

As they went round the corner the robots
came to a huge metal door that completely
blocked off the tunnel. Set in the middle was

another, much smaller door. Grunt opened this and stepped to one side.

"Da Boss is in here," said Grunt. "You will av to go on your own coz dis big door don't open."

Al peered into the darkness beyond the doorway.

He couldn't see a thing and didn't like the idea of them going through the door on their own, but there was no way Grunt could go with them. He was just too big.

"So what *is* this big door for then?" asked Al.

"It's an old flood door," said Torch. "There's lots of them in the drains and sewers beneath Metrocity. They were made years ago to stop the city from flooding."

"Flooding!" said Al. "But it has not rained here for years."

"Dat is right," said Grunt. "And most of da big doors haven't bin used for so long dat dey is stuck."

Once Torch and Al had stepped through the small doorway, Grunt closed it behind them and the two friends were left in darkness. Torch was about to turn his lamp on when a rectangle of light appeared in front of them as another door was opened and a familiar-looking robot head glared out at them.

"Da Boss will see you now," growled the robot.

Torch and Al looked at each other in amazement.

"Is that Grunt?" said Al.

Torch nodded his head. "It certainly looks like him," he said.

"It sounds like him too," agreed Torch.

"But how did he get round there so quickly?" said Al.

"Da Boss does not like to be kept waiting," growled the huge robot, stepping through the doorway.

As the robot came towards them, Torch and Al realised it wasn't Grunt after all. Grunt didn't have blue stripes painted across his face and chest, and Grunt's knuckles didn't scrape along the floor as he walked, sending up showers of sparks.

"Hey," said Al, "you look just like Grunt."

The robot stared at Al with its mouth open, revealing large square teeth, but didn't say anything.

"Anyone would think you were his brother," said Al.

The robot frowned as if deep in thought for a moment, then growled at them.

"Da Boss does not like to be kept waiting."

"Perhaps it's Grunt's *stupid big brother*," whispered Torch.

"Da Boss does not like ..."

"All right, all right," said Torch. "We're coming."

Al and Torch hurried through the door with the big robot close behind them. The door closed with a solid clang then the robot locked it and stood guard. Anyone wanting to go back through the door would have to get past the big robot first and Torch felt sure that would be a painful experience.

There were more of the big robots standing around the outside of the room guarding different doors. They all looked like Grunt too, except for the blue lines that were painted on their faces and bodies.

Torch thought the blue paint made them look like members of an ancient tribe. *And perhaps they are*, he thought. *The Mekanix.*

Then his attention was drawn to something else.

Sitting in the middle of the room, on a tangled nest of metal and wire, was the oldest-looking robot Torch had ever seen.

"Does it remind you of someone?" asked Torch.

"It looks like a ZX TK 60," whispered Al. "The same as Crank."

"And the same as the other race drivers we saw in the museum," said Al.

"SILENCE!" roared the big robot guard from behind them. "Da Boss is going to speak."

"Welcome to the Mekanix Workshop," said the Boss, spreading eight arms in welcome. "I am Pylon."

"Arghhh!" screamed Al. "You look like a spider ... What happened to your arms?"

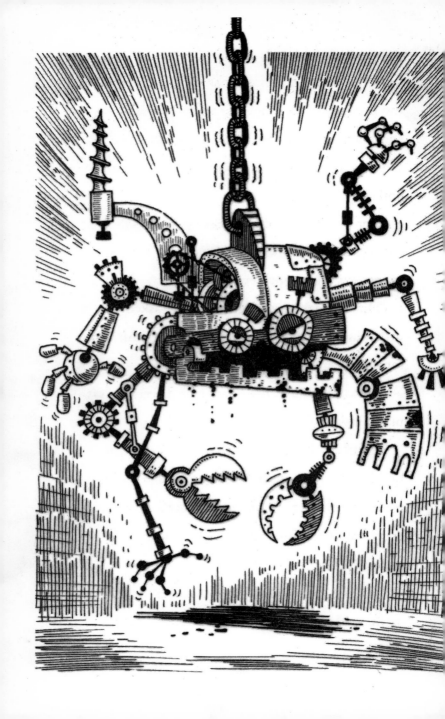

Pylon looked at his arms as if seeing them for the first time. One was long and thin. Another was short and fat. A couple of the arms had pincers on the end and one even had what looked like a giant corkscrew.

"I had a little accident," said Pylon. "The Mekanix repaired me as well as they could, but it's not easy getting the parts these days. They're always on the lookout for spares, but you're the first things to come out of the recycling plant for a long time."

"How do *you* know we came from the recycling plant?" asked Torch.

"Everything comes from the recycling plant," said Pylon. "Except the Mekanix, of course. They were here when the junk yard was still in use. But even I came from the recycling plant."

"You escaped!" said Al. "Like us?"

"That's right," said Pylon. "The Mekanix rescued me from the botweilers and brought me here."

"So how did you become their Boss?" asked Torch.

"The Mekanix have been at war with the Engineerz for many years," said Pylon, "but instead of fighting, they like to race in the tunnels.

"I helped the Mekanix design a racer that would beat the Engineerz. Then I raced it to victory and have been their leader ever since."

"What if someone else wins a race?" asked Al.

"Then they would become the new leader," said Pylon. "But the Mekanix have not won a race for a long time."

"So what if Crank beats the Engineerz?" said Al. "Will he become the new Boss?"

"It's not quite as simple as that," said Pylon,

with a smile. "You have to survive as well as win."

There was something about the way Pylon smiled that gave Al the creeps. It made him think that, win or lose, Crank was going to be in big trouble.

"So what are *we* supposed to do?" said Al.

"I'm sure you will come in useful for something," said Pylon. "But for now you should make yourself at home here at the Workshop. Grunt will take you to see your friend."

One of the big guards opened a door behind Pylon to reveal Grunt waiting patiently for them.

"Come on den," said Grunt. "You has a lot of work to do."

"Work!" said Al. "But I thought you said robots were free to do what they wanted."

"Yeah," said Grunt. "Dat is right. As long as you do what da Boss tells you."

When Al and Torch found him, Crank was lying down having his paintwork polished by two of the Mekanix, while another one was polishing a jacket.

"That will be all, thanks," said Crank. "My race team has arrived."

The Mekanix helped Crank put on his jacket and then left the room, leaving the door open for Al and Torch. As they went in through the door there was a whistling and beeping sound from behind them and Sparks came scuttling along the corridor with a spanner in one hand.

"Come in," said Crank, looking up at his friends. "How do you like my room?"

"*Your* room!" said Al. "I thought we were supposed to be looking for Robotika."

"*Robotika?*" said Crank, sounding puzzled.

"Yes, Robotika," said Al. "You know ... that place where robots are free to live their lives without having to worry about being recycled or crushed."

"*Oh*, that place," said Crank. "Well if you ask me, I think we've already found Robotika. It's not quite the way I imagined it to be, but *I* think it's great."

"*Great?*" cried Al. "What is so great about it?"

"Haven't you heard?" said Crank. "I'm the new driver. They treat me like a king. I have a room of my own and a race crew to attend to my every need ... what more could a robot ask for?"

"What about us?" said Al.

"You're my race crew, of course," said Crank.

"Your race crew?" said Al. "And *what* are you doing wearing that ridiculous jacket?"

"Great, isn't it?" said Crank, turning round to show off his jacket. It was shiny and black, with red stripes down the sleeves. The words *Champion Driver* were written in bright yellow across the back, and red flames curled up from the letter *D* to make it look even more impressive.

"And look," said Crank, "you get jackets too. They're not as cool as mine, of course. And they're a bit dusty – but they're better than nothing."

Crank pulled a couple of blue jackets out of a box and threw one each to Al and Torch before rummaging around for something else.

"Here it is," he said at last, pulling out a hat and sitting it down on top of Sparks' head.

Sparks whistled and beeped his thanks as he adjusted the cap.

"There you are," said Crank. "Even Sparks likes it here. We should at least give it a try ... what do you think?"

"I don't know," said Torch, as he tried to

squeeze into his jacket. "How does it look?"

"It looks great," said Crank, giving a big thumbs-up. "Team Crank ready for victory."

"*Team Crank?*" cried Al, looking at his jacket in disgust.

"Yes," said Crank. "Team Crank. After all ... I am the driver."

"But you have never driven a race car in your life," said Al.

"I know," said Crank. "But how hard can it be? Anyway, I'm bound to win. I am a ZX TK 60, and all the best drivers have been ZK TK 60s."

"Yes, we know," said Al, "we saw the pictures in the racing museum. Pylon is a ZX TK 60 too."

"That's right," said Crank, "*and* he's the Boss."

"But he was the first one," said Al, "and the Mekanix have not won a race since then. There have been a lot of ZX TK 60s and all that is left of them is little bits of junk."

"Don't you worry," said Crank. "I'll win the race and then *I'll* be the Boss. Then we can do whatever I want."

"I am not so sure about that," said Al. "Anyway, I do not trust Pylon. There is something he is not telling us."

"Nonsense," said Crank. "Pylon just wants to see the Mekanix win again. He knows a champion when he sees one and says that once I get behind the wheel of the Beast there will be no stopping me."

"And what about us?" asked Al. "What happens to us if you win and become the Boss of the Mekanix?"

"I'll need *someone* to help me," said Crank. "These Mekanix are all right but they just don't know how to polish a robot properly. Look! They've missed bits on my legs. Do you think you could just give it a quick rub while you're not doing anything?"

"Not doing anything!" cried Al. "NOT DOING ANYTHING! I am leaving. That is what *I* am doing."

"Leaving? But where will you go?" said Crank. "You can't go back into Metrocity or they'll take you to the recycling plant, and Pylon says that there are monsters in the wastelands out beyond the junk yard. That's why the Mekanix stay here."

"HA!" shouted Al. "*Anywhere* is better than here." And he stormed out of the room, slamming the door behind him.

"He'll be back," said Crank. "He's left his jacket behind."

Sparks whistled and beeped a reply and Torch nodded his head sadly.

"What did he say?" asked Crank.

"He said he doesn't think Al wants to be in Team Crank any more," said Torch. "And I don't blame him. Things aren't going quite the way we'd hoped, are they?"

"Of course they are," said Crank. "Everything will turn out just the way we wanted. I just need your help so I can win this race."

"Yes," agreed Torch. "You're right about that."

"There," said Crank, "I knew you'd see it my way."

"No!" said Torch. "I meant, you're right about needing our help. I think Al's right. Pylon *is* up to something ... I just don't know what it is yet."

"You worry too much," said Crank. "Why don't you have a nice relaxing oil bath?"

"No thanks," said Torch. "I'm going to go and find Al."

"Well, do you think you could fill the bath for me before you go?" asked Crank. "I've had a busy day and I need to relax before the race."

Torch didn't say anything. He just glared at Crank and headed out of the room, leaving him alone with Sparks.

"If you ask me," said Crank, "someone is jealous that *they* weren't picked to be the driver."

Sparks examined the spanner in his hand and headed off back towards the Mekanix garage without saying anything.

After leaving Crank's room, Al wandered along the
passageways and tunnels that made up the
Mekanix Workshop. He had no idea where most
of the passages went but he didn't really care
either. He just needed to get away from Crank for
a while.

"Team Crank!" Al grumbled to himself. Crank
was supposed to be the smart one. How could he
be so stupid as to believe a single word that Pylon
had said? And even if Crank *did* manage to beat
the Engineerz in a race, Al was sure that Pylon
wouldn't let him become the Boss.

Al couldn't help remembering the way Pylon

had smiled when he'd said that *it wasn't enough to win the race — you had to survive as well*. He didn't know what Pylon had meant by that, but he felt positive it would spell bad news for Crank and the rest of them.

The tunnel Al was walking along was getting darker by the minute. He didn't like the look of it, but wasn't quite ready to go back and join *Team Crank* just yet. He was sure the others thought he was a useless robot that didn't know anything … Well, he'd show them. He'd find out what Pylon was up to and get them out of this place if it was the last thing he did.

A little further on, Al discovered that the tunnel opened up into what looked like a room, but it was hard to see anything properly as it was so dark. He was about to investigate further when huge overhead bulbs blinked into life, flooding everything with light.

In the bright light, Al saw it wasn't really a

room at all, but a huge chamber between two much larger tunnels. The mouth of one of the tunnels had been boarded over with wooden planks but the other one stood open.

Al could see it disappearing round a bend in the distance. Hanging above the mouth of the tunnel, on lengths of chain, were two huge vid-screens. They looked out of place in the large chamber and Al couldn't help wondering why they were there.

Standing near the middle of the chamber were two huge pillars supporting the roof. Metal ladders ran up the side of each pillar and disappeared into the shadows far above. For a moment, Al wondered whether they might provide a way out … but for now, his attention was drawn to the bottom of the pillars, where huge chains were fastened. The chains fastened to one of the pillars lay in a heap on the floor, but those on the pillar closest to

him were fastened to the back of a race car.

This wasn't the Mekanix Beast they'd seen earlier in the garage, this was another car. Painted red and black, this car was smaller than the Beast, but it looked fast and powerful. Al was about to take a closer look when a door opened at the far side of the chamber and the sound of robot voices reached his ears.

"Are you sure it's ready?" said one of the voices.

"Yes, Boss," said another voice. "*You* will have full control of the racer *and* you will be able to see it perfectly on your vid-screen. It will feel like you're driving it yourself, but no one will guess that the tunnel racer isn't being driven by the Engineerz."

Al quickly hid himself behind the closest pillar as the two robots came into the chamber. One of them was Pylon, the Mekanix Boss, walking on his eight arms like a giant metal spider, but Al didn't recognise the second robot.

Peeking out from behind the pillar, Al tried to get a better view. At first he thought the second robot must be one of the Mekanix, but there was something different about this robot that he couldn't quite work out at first. Then it came to him …

The Mekanix were all painted blue. Even the big robot guards had blue stripes on them – but this robot was red and black like the race car. This robot was definitely not one of the Mekanix. And that could only mean one thing. This must be one of the Engineerz. But what was Pylon doing here with one of the Engineerz *and* their racer?

"It's dangerous meeting here before the race," said the Engineer. "If anyone found out they would—"

"Don't worry about anyone else," hissed Pylon. "They are all preparing for tomorrow's race. The Mekanix are so sure they will finally beat the Engineerz."

"But the Engineerz are already beaten," cried the robot. "We don't have enough parts to keep building tunnel racers and keep ourselves repaired. We have to stop the races."

"Yes," said Pylon. "Sad, isn't it. But this will be the final and most terrible race ever. There will be an unfortunate crash and both the racers and the drivers will be destroyed. There will be no more races – which should make the Engineerz happy.

And I will be able to stop worrying about the Mekanix finding a new champion. I've got used to being the Boss around here."

Al could hardly believe his hearing circuits. Pylon was planning to destroy both of the racers just to stop anyone else becoming the Boss. That must have been what he meant by *it wasn't enough just to win the race* ...

He would have to get back and warn Crank.

"But what about me?" asked the Engineer.

"I said you would be free once I was certain the Engineerz tunnel racer was ready," said Pylon. "And I always keep my promise."

"Well, here's the Engineerz tunnel racer," said the Engineer. "Just as you ordered."

"Yes," said Pylon, "and it looks perfect. But there is just *one* thing before I let you go."

"And what is that?" asked the Engineer.

"This car needs a driver," said Pylon.

"A driver?" squeaked the Engineer. "But who

would be mad enough to ride in a car they know is going to be destroyed?"

"Who indeed," said Pylon as he grabbed the Engineer and lifted it into the air.

The Engineer kicked and wriggled trying to get out of Pylon's grasp, but it was no use. Blue sparks crackled around its body and smoke snaked out from its joints as Pylon crushed it between two of his deadly pincers.

When he'd finished, Pylon dropped the Engineer into the seat of the racer and pushed a helmet on to its head.

"There," said Pylon, "I said I'd set you free. Now you'll never have to worry about spare parts again."

From his hiding place, Al watched in horror as Pylon scuttled across the chamber and disappeared down the tunnel, leaving him alone with the life-less Engineer and the tunnel racer.

8

"I've searched all over the place," said Torch. "I've even been back to the Mekanix Racing Museum, but there's no sign of Al anywhere. Grunt says the Engineerz might have got him."

"Well, I don't know what the Engineerz would want him for," said Crank.

"Spare parts, of course," said Torch. "Grunt says the Engineerz and the Mekanix are running out of spare parts and they'd like nothing better than to get their hands on a new robot like Al."

"They wouldn't do that to another robot, would they?" said Crank.

"Of course they would," said Torch. "Look what

the Tin Man did to Al in the recycling plant."

Crank would never forget what the Tin Man had done. Finding Al ready to be crushed, with his legs torn off, had been terrible. It was something Crank didn't want to have to think about ever again … but surely the Engineerz weren't like the Tin Man.

"I bet he's just hiding somewhere," said Crank. "He's jealous that I'm the one that was chosen to be the driver. He'll be back, just you wait and see."

"I hope you're right," said Torch.

"Of course I am," said Crank. "When have I *ever* been wrong?"

Before Torch could answer, Grunt burst in through the door.

"Da Boss sez it's time for da race," growled Grunt. "Your car is ready … come on."

"And about time too," said Crank. "I'm tired of all this waiting around. Let's get going."

Grunt led the way down to the garage, where the Mekanix tunnel racer stood waiting for them. It was the first time any of them had seen the racer since it had been finished, and it looked amazing.

"Just look at it," said Crank. "It's fantastic."

"It *is* good," agreed Torch.

"It is Da Beast," said Grunt, nodding his head in appreciation. "Now let's get pushing."

"Pushing!" cried Crank.

"Of course," said Grunt. "You can't drive Da Beast down the tunnels to the chamber. It goes too fast."

"Couldn't I just drive slowly?" asked Crank.

"Slowly?" said Grunt in disgust. "Da Beast does not do slowly. It only does fast and very fast."

The Beast was big and heavy and the tunnels were long and narrow, but eventually they made it to the chamber. As they pushed it in through one of the side doors a loud cheer came up from the crowd of Mekanix that had gathered to watch the race.

"DRIVER, DRIVER, DRIVER," they roared.

"Hey," said Crank. "There's Sparks standing with the other Mekanix. You'd think he would come and help us push instead of just standing there."

"Nah," growled Grunt. "Pushing is da job of the da race crew. All da Mekanix has to do now is watch da race and pick up da pieces."

"Pick up the pieces?" said Crank. "What pieces?"

"Your pieces of course," said Grunt. "Da Mekanix drivers always ends up in pieces."

"Well not this driver," said Crank. "This driver's going to win the race and come back in *one* piece. Even the Boss said there would be no stopping me."

"Yeah," said Grunt. "Dat is always da problem."

"What problem?" said Crank, starting to feel a little worried. "No one said anything to me about a problem."

"Don't worry," said Torch. "Sparks told me that he has made a few little improvements to the Beast ... though he did wonder why there was no—"

"No time to worry about dat," interrupted Grunt. "Da Boss is ready to start da race."

The two vid-screens hanging above the mouth of the tunnel flickered into life and two giant images of Pylon's face stared down at everyone. The only sound in the chamber was the clang and rattle of chains as Grunt fastened the back of the Beast up to one of the huge pillars. Everyone else silently watched the vid-screens as they waited for Pylon to speak.

"Drivers …" Pylon's voice boomed from the loudspeakers, "… to your racers."

Crank could see that the driver of the Engineerz tunnel racer was already in his seat. He'd been there all the time and Crank hadn't even seen him move. *Probably nervous*, thought Crank, *knowing he's having to race against me.*

Crank was snapped from his thoughts as Grunt slapped a helmet on to his head. "Don't forget dis," growled Grunt.

"Why do I need a helmet?" said Crank, peering out from beneath the visor. "My head's made of metal."

"Trust me," said Grunt. "You needs a helmet."

No sooner had Grunt spoken than four of the Mekanix rushed forward and lifted Crank into the air.

"Arghh!" cried Crank, waving his arms about. "I can do it myself, you know!"

The four Mekanix carried Crank across to the Beast and dropped him into the seat. Then they started fastening all the seat belts around him.

"Ouch!" yelled Crank. "Watch what you're doing … that's much too tight."

The Mekanix ignored him and carried on tightening the straps until Crank could hardly move.

"Dey is to stop you gettin' out," said Grunt.

"You mean they are to stop me *falling* out," said Crank.

"Yeah," said Grunt. "Dat as well."

Crank pushed the visor up on his helmet and turned to look at the driver of the Engineerz tunnel racer. He was still staring straight forward.

"Good luck," shouted Crank, but the driver ignored him. All Crank could see of the Engineerz driver was a red helmet and that hadn't even moved when he'd shouted.

How rude, thought Crank. *It's no wonder the Mekanix don't like the Engineerz.*

There was nothing Crank could do other than sit and wait. He glanced up at the vid-screens that hung from the walls and saw images of two drivers. One showed the red helmet and dark visor of the Engineerz while the other showed a frightened-looking robot face staring at the camera. It took Crank a moment to realise that the face on the screen was his.

Crank gave a little wave and tried his best to smile and look confident.

After all, he thought, *it's only a race. It can't be that bad . . .*

. . . can it?

9

Crank sat at the wheel of the Beast and tried to relax, but he was starting to get a bad feeling about the race and couldn't stop fidgeting in his seat. Thankfully, the camera had turned away, so at least he wouldn't have to look at his own worried face on the vid-screen any more.

Looking around, Crank saw the large chamber was almost full of robots now. Even Pylon's big guards had come to watch the race. The only ones not there seemed to be Al and Pylon himself.

Crank was disappointed Al hadn't turned up. He'd felt sure he would come for the race. Although he didn't like to admit it, Crank was starting to worry about him … *What if the Engineerz have got him*, he thought. *What if they're pulling him apart right now while I'm just sitting here?*

Then a voice called out to him.

"Crank! … Over here."

Crank looked round and was surprised to see the driver of the Engineerz tunnel racer waving at him. What was even more surprising was that the driver was Al. Crank could hardly believe his eyes … Al, racing for the Engineerz. The traitor.

"What are you doing?" cried Crank. "I thought you were my *friend*."

"I *am* your friend," shouted Al, "but I am stuck."

"STUCK," yelled Crank. "Oh, I bet you're stuck. You should have thought of that before you joined the enemy."

"The Engineerz are not the enemy," shouted Al. "It is Pylon. He is going to …"

But Al's words were drowned out as the engines of the two tunnel racers roared into life and the chains holding them to the pillars pulled tight.

Al was still shouting, trying to make himself heard over the noise of the engines, but Crank ignored him.

If Al wants a race, thought Crank, easing his foot on to the accelerator pedal, *then Al's going to get a race.* The Beast's engines gave a mighty growl and smoke rose from the tyres as they squealed and spun on the floor, trying to get a grip. Only the thick chains stopped the racer from speeding off down the tunnel.

This feels good, thought Crank, revving the engine. *I'll show them who's the best driver.*

CRACK

Something whacked against the side of Crank's helmet, nearly knocking his head off. His foot slipped from the accelerator pedal and the roar of the engine dropped to a growl.

"What do you think you're doing?" snarled a voice in his ear.

Crank straightened his helmet and looked round into the angry face of one of the Mekanix.

"You're going to burn the tyres out messing around like that," roared the robot, waving a spanner in his face.

Crank felt the side of his head where the spanner had hit him, putting a big dent in the helmet. *Grunt was right*, he thought. *I did need the helmet after all.*

A sudden cheer from the crowd made Crank look up. Pylon's face had returned and was glaring out from both vid-screens.

"Are ... You ... Ready?" boomed Pylon's voice from the speakers.

Crank nodded his head weakly and gripped the steering wheel. *At least the tunnel racer will be easy to drive*, he thought. *With only a steering wheel and an accelerator pedal, I'm not likely to get things muddled up.*

"Then release the racers," boomed Pylon.

Another loud cheer came from the crowd as two huge robot guards stepped forward. The engines from the tunnel racers roared louder and smoke rose from the tyres as they pulled against the holding chains.

At exactly the same instant, the two robot guards bit through the thick chains and the tunnel racers shot forwards ...

The race was on.

A line of lights in the roof illuminated the

tunnel ahead of them as the two racers sped off side by side. Crank felt himself being pushed back into his seat and the walls of the tunnel became a blur as the Beast picked up speed.

From the corner of his eye Crank caught sight of the red and black tunnel racer moving ahead of him as they approached the first corner. Crank pressed harder on the accelerator and the Beast roared ahead, riding high up on the tunnel wall and shooting round the bend into first place.

The Engineerz racer hurtled round the corner right behind Crank, then rode along the side of the tunnel before speeding past to take the lead once more.

As the racer went past, Crank caught a glimpse of Al in the driver seat. He was still waving his arms in the air and shouting, though Crank had no idea what he was trying to say.

He must be mad, thought Crank, *messing around while he's driving as fast as that.*

Up ahead was a dark patch in the tunnel, but it wasn't until the speeding cars got closer that Crank realised just what made it so dark. Part of the tunnel had collapsed and fallen into a huge hole, leaving a wide gap in their path.

Crank pressed the accelerator pedal as far as it would go and the Beast shot forwards,

pushing him back into the seat.

As the Beast flew across the gap, Crank closed his eyes and gripped the steering wheel until a heavy jolt told him he'd landed on the other side. The Beast swerved when it hit the ground and Crank was struggling to keep control when something crashed against the side of him.

Looking round, Crank saw it had been the Engineerz tunnel racer and was amazed to see that Al was now riding on the *front* of it. What *did* he think he was doing?

Crank shook his head in wonder as Al clambered back into the driver's seat just as the two racers flew round another corner.

The two cars sped along, side by side, neither one quite managing to get past the other, when Crank saw something that made his mouth drop open in horror.

The wide tunnel they were racing along suddenly changed up ahead. Crank's side of the tunnel became a solid wall while the other side became very narrow, wide enough for just one of the racers. They would have to drive one in front of the other if they were going to get through.

Crank pressed his foot on the accelerator pedal, hoping to overtake Al, but it made no difference. The Beast was already going as fast as it could.

There was only one thing he could do, so Crank stamped on the brake pedal as hard as he could, before remembering there was no brake pedal. Pylon had been right, there *would* be no stopping him.

Looking round in desperation, Crank saw Al frantically waving his arms around and pointing at the Engineerz tunnel racer.

That's it, he thought. *My last chance of escape.*

Struggling to release his safety straps, Crank clambered out of his seat and on to the front of the Beast. The paintwork was smooth and polished, and Crank slithered around for a moment before managing to get his balance.

Crank looked at the ground rushing beneath the wheels of the two racers. If he fell, they'd be sweeping his bits up for days, but if he stayed where he was he'd be smashed against the tunnel wall.

There was only one thing for it ...

Crank leaped across the gap and landed heavily on the Engineerz tunnel racer just as the Beast hit the wall. The sound of the explosion rattled through the tunnels but Crank was long gone ... desperately hanging on to the front of the red and black racer as it hurtled along the narrow tunnel.

Crank had managed to escape from the exploding Beast, but he didn't know how he was going to get off the front of the Engineerz racer. He could feel himself slipping towards one of the front wheels when a hand reached out to him.

"Here!" said Al. "Let me help you …"

Crank grabbed his hand and Al pulled him on to the top of the racer where they sat for a moment as the walls of the tunnel raced by.

"Thanks for lending a hand," said Crank. "That wheel was getting a bit too close for comfort."

"Any time," said Al. "I was not doing anything anyway."

"Not doing anything?" said Crank. "You're doing a pretty good job of driving this ..."

Crank stopped talking and looked past Al towards the driver's seat. "Wait a minute," he said. "If you're sat here with me, then who's driving this thing?"

"Do not worry," said Al. "Pylon is driving."

"Pylon's driving ...?" cried Crank. "What's he doing driving the Engineerz tunnel racer?"

"That is what I was *trying* to tell you at the start of the race," said Al. "Pylon destroyed the Engineerz leader and is controlling the whole race. He is planning a huge crash so there will be no more races and no more champions."

"So how did you end up in the race?" said Crank.

"I had to warn you about what Pylon was up to, but got trapped in the chamber," said Al. "I needed somewhere to hide until you came in for the race and the only place I could think of was in the racer itself … but I got stuck and did not manage to get free until after we jumped over that hole."

"I thought you were just messing about!"

"Messing about!" said Al. "I nearly fell out."

"It could've been worse," said Crank. "At least we've put a stop to Pylon's plans."

"It is worse," said Al. "Pylon is going to crash this racer too, so that no one will know what he has been up to."

"Then we've got to stop it," said Crank, crawling along the top of the racer.

"It is no use," said Al. "Pylon has control."

"I'll soon see about that," said Crank, dropping into the seat and grabbing the steering wheel.

Crank was relieved to find the Engineerz tunnel racer had been fitted with two pedals. An accelerator and a brake. But when he stamped his foot on to the brake pedal his relief turned to panic. Nothing happened and the red and black racer kept speeding along the tunnel.

"I can't control it," cried Crank.

"I know," said Al, patiently. "That is because Pylon is controlling it."

"WE'RE GOING TO CRASH!" screamed Crank at the top of his voice.

Al was about to answer when the red and black racer suddenly swerved to the left and started climbing the side of the tunnel.

"Arghh!" cried Al, trying to keep a hold of the racer as it swerved to the right and climbed the wall at the other side of the tunnel.

"What's happening?" cried Crank.

"I think this is where we crash," shouted Al.

The racer steadied itself just in time to speed round a tight bend in the tunnel, then a loud squealing sound came from the back wheels and the smell of burning rubber filled the air.

"It's the brakes," cried Crank, as the racer started to skid along the tunnel.

For an instant, he saw something standing in

front of them in the middle of the tunnel, then the racer came to a sudden halt and Crank and Al found themselves flying through the air.

There was a loud crunch as Crank hit the floor, then a groan from beneath him. He'd landed on Al.

"Nice to see you boys," growled a voice from above.

Crank slowly looked up and saw a huge robot standing above him. It was Grunt. Standing behind him were Torch and Sparks.

"What ... what happened?" said Crank, getting shakily to his feet.

"I put da brakes on," said Grunt.

"But I thought Pylon was controlling the Engineerz racer," said Crank.

"He woz," said Grunt, holding up a small box. "He woz using dis."

"A remote control," said Al. "But how did you get it?"

"Pylon dropped it when I jumped on 'im," said Grunt, proudly.

"You *jumped* on him?" cried Crank.

"It was very messy," said Torch. "Spare parts everywhere."

"Spare parts?" said Al.

"Well," said Grunt. "Dey is spare now. Hur ... hur ... hur."

Torch explained that Sparks had found the broken body of the Engineer that Al had hidden in the chamber, so they'd gone to tell Pylon that something was wrong.

"That's when we discovered that Pylon was behind it all, and that he was controlling the race," said Torch.

"And dat's when I jumped on him," said Grunt. "Den we came to help you."

"What are we going to do now?" asked Crank.

"We should get out of here," said Torch. "The Engineerz and the Mekanix won't be happy when they find out what's happened."

"But it was not our fault," said Al.

"Dey won't worry about dat," said Grunt. "You destroyed one tunnel racer and you stealing da other one."

"That's ridiculous," cried Crank. "We're not stealing it."

"Yes you are," said Grunt, clambering on top of

the red and black tunnel racer. "It's da only way to get out of da junk yard and we'd better get going."

The robots turned and saw a crowd of Mekanix and Engineerz charging up the tunnel towards them … And they *didn't* look happy.

Jumping into the driver's seat, Crank started the engine while the others clambered aboard.

When they were ready, Sparks started whistling and beeping at them.

"What did he say?" said Crank.

"He said get going," said Torch.

"But he's not on board yet."

"Sparks says he's not coming," said Torch. "He's got some ideas for a new tunnel racer he wants to try out."

"What?" cried Crank. "We can't leave him here!"

"Sparks likes it here," said Torch. "He's happy working on the tunnel racers."

"Yeah," said Grunt. "An' fings will be different around here now that Pylon's gone."

"Are you sure he'll be all right?" said Crank.

"Yes," said Torch. "Sparks helped finish building the Beast ... it's us they don't like. Now GO!"

Crank didn't need telling twice. As the crowd of Mekanix and Engineerz came closer, Crank pressed his foot on to the accelerator and the huge racer shot forwards down the tunnel. Mekanix and Engineerz threw themselves to either side as the racer thundered towards them.

"Which way?" shouted Crank above the noise of the engine.

"To da Wastelands," shouted Grunt.

"But didn't the Boss say there were monsters in the Wastelands?"

"Yeah ... but 'e woz probably tellin' fibs," growled Grunt. "Da Boss told lots o' dem."

The tunnel racer shot out of the tunnel and flew across the starting chamber before crashing through the wooden boards that covered the mouth of the other tunnel.

A little way ahead, daylight was streaming in and in no time at all the tunnel racer had left the tunnels beneath Metrocity and was speeding along an old concrete waterway that was once used to carry water to the city.

"Now where do we go?" shouted Crank.

"Torch sez dare is a place called Robotika," said Grunt. "A place where all robots are free to do what dey wants. Grunt fink we should go dare."

"I think you're right," said Crank. "Let's go."

Crank pressed his foot down on the accelerator

and the red and black racer sped off along the waterway, leaving Metrocity and the junk yard far behind.

The big tunnel racer thundered along the old waterway, throwing up clouds of dust, until it came to a place where the way was blocked. A bridge, stretching from one side to the other, had collapsed many years before leaving the way blocked by huge chunks of concrete and rusted metal. There was no way of getting past so Crank had to drive round it.

Beyond the broken bridge, the waterway was cracked and full of wreckage so the four robots had to continue their journey across the hard desert ground of the Wastelands.

The Wastelands were hot and dry, and the ground was littered with the bones of dead animals and all sorts of wreckage. It was hard driving and Crank had to be extra careful not to bump into anything.

"Everything is dead," said Al.

"Fings die here very quick," said Grunt. "Dis is not a good place to be. We should head for da mountains. Perhaps we will find Robotika there."

Crank turned the tunnel racer towards the mountains and pressed his foot down on the accelerator.

As they sped across the Wastelands, the four robot friends were all so busy looking forward that none of them noticed the little cloud of dust that was following them . A cloud of dust that had been following them since they'd left the junk yard.

The End

CRANK

AL

SPARKS

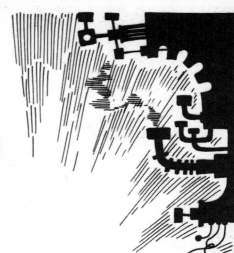

TORCH

book 3

Razorbites

"Scavengers," said Grunt, pointing at the glowing eyes as he clambered back down on to the racer.

Torch opened his mouth to reply but as he did so a loud explosion shook the air and a cloud of smoke rose up from further back along the convoy.

The four friends stood up and tried to see what was happening, but the land cruiser behind them was so close it blocked out most of the view.

Then there was a shout …

"STOP THEM!"

It was Quill. He was up on top of the land cruiser with Bouncer, pointing at something.

As Crank and the others turned to see what it was, three robots ran into view, tripping over rocks and stumbling in their effort to get across the dried riverbed.

One of the robots looked back at Crank and the others …

"RUN!" cried the robot. "Run for your lives."

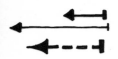

DAMIAN HARVEY

  lives in Blackpool with his wife and three daughters, their four cats, a horde of guinea pigs, a tank full of fish and a quirky imaginatio

He loves music, movies, reading, swimming, walking, cheese and ice cream – but not always at the same time.

Before realising how much fun he could have writing and making thin up he worked as a lifeguard, had a job in a boring office and once save the galaxy from invading vampire robots (though none of these were a exciting as they sound).

Damian now spends lots of time in front of his computer but loves getting out to visit schools and libraries to share stories, talk about writing and get people excited about books.